The Mercantile

Larry Rhodes

The Mercantile

Olympia Publishers
London

www.olympiapublishers.com
OLYMPIA PAPERBACK EDITION

A CIP catalogue record for this title is
available from the British Library.

ISBN: 978-1-80439-250-8

First Published in 2023

Olympia Publishers
Tallis House
2 Tallis Street
London
EC4Y 0AB

Printed in Great Britain

Dedication

I dedicate this book to my mother who passed away in 2021.

1

Hi, stranger. What can I getcha? We don't get many visitors here in this little town of Playnesville. Just passing through? Never mind the people here, they're just regular folks. They may seem a little strange to outsiders but they're harmless. My name's William or Billy if you prefer. This here pub is the local watering hole for some of the locals. You may have noticed a sign off the side of the road reading 'The Mercantile: General Store' on your way into this town next to the burnt down husk of a building that used to be there as well. I got some stories to tell ya about that place. You're not in a rush to leave, are you? I'll tell ya what, you sit and listen to my story and the drinks would be on the house. After the Second World War ended a young man named Ira Busby had that store built outside of town and got into the retail business. Mind you, there is a local store here in town though. He did good for many years. He didn't take no shit from anyone. He was killed some time ago by a robbery gone wrong. One of his kids took over the store soon after but strange things were happening there. Well, there is some weird shit going on in this town but not that bad, it's kind of normal for us who lived here all our lives. But the things that was going on at that place made the person close up shop for good. It didn't end there though. I started having vivid dreams soon after. They were so real as if I was actually there witnessing what was happening there at the store. Even though the store was never opened at night a few people had said that they saw it open late at night after it was closed down. Nothing here in this town is ever open at night except for the travel lodge. The interior lights were on, items appeared to be stocked on the shelves, and an elderly gentleman at the register. There were a few times where there were some people seen in the little store shopping. There was always a green 1948 Studebaker M15A pickup sitting in the parking lot next to the store at night when it appeared to be opened. That was the type of truck that old Mr. Busby used to drive back in the days.

2

The first night I had the dream it wasn't long after The Mercantile was closed down for good. I watched a guy walked into the store. The shop was well lit and stocked with some grocery items, candy, snacks and drinks. The place looked clean and organized. The only other person there was the older man behind the counter at the register. He wasn't paying much attention to the young guy who came in. The "customer" was browsing around and watching the old man. Something told me that the guy was up to no good, but I wasn't able to tell the old guy. I could only watch the events play out in the dream. The younger man went to the back behind the shelves to where the alcohol was located out of sight of the old man. Looking back in the direction of the old cashier the young man grabbed hold of a case of beer then sped walked between the shelving units and the freezer toward the front entrance. I noticed the old man did nothing but stood there behind the counter near the register and watched the guy leave out with the case. I saw a bit of a smirk and glint in the old man's eyes, but it looked more sinister to me as the young guy left out. As soon as the guy stepped outside, he looked around confused as it was really foggy. It wasn't foggy when he went into the store but even though the light from inside illuminated the outside, he was only able to see about a foot or two. The young man looked about him and couldn't see his car anywhere and when he looked back to where the old man is he saw the cashier waived at him before the older gentleman evaporated into thin air. The young guy looked perplexed as he couldn't believe what he just saw and soon after the items on the shelves started to disappear as well. The florescent lights started to flicker before cutting off leaving the guy in total darkness. It was then that I woke up from my slumber. Later that day some young woman came into this pub and was asking about her boyfriend trying to find out if anybody had seen him. She also mentioned something about her car being missing. Lucky for her, the local sheriff was up in here at that time. He asked her if she owned a Honda Accord of which she said yes. He told her that it was found abandoned in the parking lot of the closed down store just outside of town. Not knowing where her boyfriend could have gone, she decided to get her car back and leave without him, figuring he may have taken off with some other woman.

3

Well, I don't have many dreams about the store except when something bad happens. There have been times where some people have been seen inside that Mercantile and nothing happened to them. Those people were good honest folks. Always the same truck would be seen in the parking lot next to the store. Some of the older folks here in this town would recognize the cashier. They knew the place was haunted. The locals stayed away from there. A few weeks later I had another dream.

4

I was inside the store looking out the large bay windows and it was real late at night when I saw two car loads of people come to the store. As they got out of the vehicles, they seemed to be a little on the drunk side. Now I have never been to college but those who went into the store looked to be college kids to me. There were five guys and four girls. Maybe they were just out on a trip to some place. They were loud and obnoxious while browsing the store all the while the old man behind the counter watched them. The way the young men and women were acting I had a bad feeling that something was gonna happen to those people and not in a good way either. Two of the girls went up to the counter where the old man was and tried to talk to him. I'm guessing they were trying to distract him while the others were up to no good but from what I could tell from the look on the man's face is that he knew what was going on. The two other girls managed to find the restroom and entered while the guys split up looking at the items on the shelves and the drinks as well. While I was watching some of the college boys start to put some items in their pockets, I overheard the conversation of the two girls at the counter with the old man.

"How are you doing tonight?" asked one of the girls.

In a slow drawl of his voice, he said, "I'm doin' just fine. Y'all girls ain't gettin' into any trouble, are ya? Don't want to see ya cajolin' with the wrong crowd." As he said that I saw his eyes looked over at one of the girls and she became a little nervous.

The other girl said, "No, sir, we're not" while giving a sly smile. The girl who got nervous said she was going outside for a bit needing some fresh air and the other argued with her some before she said, "Whatever."

As the one who became nervous about what was going on left out The Mercantile, the other girl turned around and the old guy said to her, "Y'all shouldn't be doin' what you're doin'. There are consequences to your actions."

"Whatever, old man," she shot back then proceeded toward where some of the boys were.

I felt a dread at that moment as if something terrible was gonna happen and I tried to yell out to those college kids to get out, but I wasn't producing any sound at all. As the girl reached one of the boys there was a loud scream coming from the restroom and at the same time a snarling growl with barking was emanating from the same room. Immediately one of the girls who went into the small room came running out with fear in her eyes and screaming for someone to help her. Everybody in the store turned to look in her direction except for the old man who was just standing there near the register. A moment later a large hairy mongrel dog came out of the small restroom tearing the door off its hinges and barreled toward the girl knocking her to the ground. The others including me were frozen in our place where we stood looking at it. I could see blood on its muzzle as it turned to face the other people. With quick speed the dog tore into the young college kids before anyone had a chance to do anything. I could not believe how fast the thing went and how bloody the place got. I turned to look at the old man and to my surprise he looked at me and winked with a grin on his face. I then looked back toward the large windows, and I could see the girl outside standing by one of the cars the group came in. She must have had earphones in because she never reacted to all the yelling and screaming that was going on. Then one of the guys ran right through me toward the doors and when he left out, he disappeared into the darkness without a trace. At that moment the lights within dimmed and the girl looked back towards the building with a confused look. She saw door swinging back closed and she took a step toward the building. I turned around to look at the old man, but he was nowhere to be seen and everything within the store was disappearing. The old store was reverting back to what it was before and as the girl walked in, the lights flickered off and I tried to warn her to leave the place, but I wasn't able to produce any sound. She walked through the place calling out to the others then she tripped over something that was on the ground and looked to see what it was. From what I could tell she had the look of horror on her face after she was looking at whatever it was on the floor for awhile. Then a growling was emanating from the back of the store, and she turned to look in that direction while slowly backing up. I could see a large dark shape come into view and I knew it had to be that dog. The growling became louder, and the girl took off out the door to the outside, but she didn't disappear like the college boy did. She ran past the cars toward the street and on to this here town. It was then I woke up drenched in sweat. Later that afternoon I overheard that there was a gruesome murder that took place at the old, abandoned store and a college girl was in hysterics at the sheriff's office. Apparently, the local sheriff had to get a forensic team to come in from another town to bag the bodies or what was left of them anyways. Some days later I heard that one of the college boys who was with them wasn't among the dead, but he was reported as a missing person. In this town people tend to talk and I tend to listen.

5

Nothing major happened for weeks and I was able to sleep without any nightmares plaguing me. There were still some cases where a few good people ended up at that store late at night stopping in to get some snacks and drinks before heading out to their destination. Those people were not from around here. There were talks, in hushed tones of course, that the old man's dog tore those college kids up. You know what the weird thing is? Mr. Busby's old mongrel died sometime before he died. Just when I thought the nightmares had ended, I had another dream.

6

It was close to midnight when I finally went to bed and I fell asleep as soon as my head hit the pillow and immediately after, I started having those dreams. Those dreams always have me at that damn store. This time it started with me outside in the parking lot. As I looked around the old store was open with the lights on. That old green truck was out there, and the old man was inside as usual. I then heard some voices off in the distance, but I wasn't able to understand what was being said. I turned to the direction where the voices were coming from and in the darkness, I could faintly see about three figures in the distance coming toward the convenience store. As they got closer, I recognized one of them. The man's name was Richard Bachman, and he was a homeless hermit who lived mostly in the woods or wherever he laid his head. Everyone here in Playnesville knew of him but where he came from or what he did before, no one knew. The closer they got I could hear what they were saying.

"I'm telling you – you don't want to get Mr. Busby mad at you," Richard said.

"It'll be fine, home boy," one of the others said.

"Yeah, it's going to be okay," some woman had said.

I only noticed three guys up until they got closer to me that I saw a woman behind the three. The two men who were with Richard was black and the woman was white. They appeared to be homeless and as they got closer seemed to be druggies. Those three must not be from around here as I didn't recognize any of them.

"We're just going to get a few things to tide us over. It'll be cool," one of the other men said.

"All right, just don't make him mad," Richard said. They walked right by me and entered the store. All of a sudden, I happened to be inside the store when I was outside of it. I can't explain how that happened, but you should know how dreams go.

"Hello, Richard, who's your new friends?" the old man asked.

"Oh, I just met them, Mr. Busby."

"Did you now?" The old man's eyes gazed at the three who came in with Richard. The woman I noticed put on what seemed like a fake smile while walking by going around to where the soda fountain was located while one of the men walked around looking at the snacks on the shelves. I noticed what the woman was wearing as she was walking, me being a guy you know. She had on one of those tight full body miniskirts which the bottom of her ass was showing. No matter how much she pulled it down to cover herself, it kept riding up revealing more of her plump ass. I couldn't tell if she had thongs on or not as her skirt didn't move up that far before she started pulling it down some. I saw that the guy who was looking around kept eyeing old Mr. Busby. The other guy was at the counter smiling and talking nonsense. I guess he was trying to distract the old man, but Mr. Busby wasn't stupid. Richard looked to be a little nervous standing there by the counter and the old man noticed that. Apparently, the woman had gotten herself a drink as I heard ice being dropped into a cup then the soda fountain made a noise indicating that one of the drinks was pouring into the cup. Old Mr. Busby didn't pay any attention to what she was doing. Then the woman snuck over to the cold sandwich case and looked at the items in it. I couldn't help but look at her back side as I am a man after all. I did notice that she stopped trying to pull her skirt down as the bottom of it was halfway up her ass. As she bent over to look at something on the bottom shelf, I saw that she wasn't wearing any undies as I could see her hairy twat. Standing back up she snagged a couple of sandwiches and proceeded to eat onc while looking over her shoulder at the old man. I couldn't tell what the other guy was doing but I could hazard a guess that he was stuffing his pockets with snacks.

Old Mr. Busby turned to look at Richard and said, "I like you, Richard, I really do. Don't you think you need to be doing something right about now?"

"Nothing I can think of," Richard replied.

"I really do think that you need to go and take care of what you need to take care of." Old man Busby had that look that said you need to leave cause things are about to get bad.

Richard then smiled nervously then said, "Come to think of it, I do need to take care of something."

"You ain't gotta leave, man. He can't make you leave," the guy at the counter said to Richard.

"That's okay, I need to go, sorry," Richard quickly said then walked out the store as fast as he could going right through me.

That homeless man watched Richard leave out then turned to look at old Mr. Busby. At that time the woman was walking around toward the front where the guy was standing near Mr. Busby then stopped all of a sudden holding her stomach. "Oh, gawd, my stomach," she cried out.

The guy who was rummaging through the snacks

started toward her hollering, "What the fuck's wrong with you, bitch?" It sounded like he had something in his mouth. Apparently, he was eating something he had gotten off from one of the shelves. The woman looked at him and before she could say a word, she threw up all over the floor. The bile looked sickly green in color.

"The shit? What the fuck you ate, girl?" the guy at the counter asked. Old man Mr. Busby eyed me with a smile and winked. Without saying another word, she up chucked again and the look on her face told me she was hurting.

"You fucking cunt, you done shit yourself!" The other guy said. It was then I noticed a stream of something brown running down her legs from her tight miniskirt. Her legs apparently weren't able to support her as she went down on her hands and knees. She continued to vomit and the way she was bending over, her miniskirt moved up over her ass and I could see shit spray out onto the floor.

The guy who was going through the aisles grabbing stuff looked over at Mr. Busby angrily. "Fucking old man, you poisoned her!" He took two steps toward the counter then doubled over grasping his stomach. The one at the counter near Mr. Busby was looking back and forth between him and the two he came in with. His eyes were wide open as he was in shock and couldn't believe what was going on.

He then covered his nose as he said, "That fucking stinks."

The guy who was doubled over cried out, "Help me, man!" before puking his guts out. I saw tears coming down his face then he said, "I shit myself." Then he vomited again. Whatever those two ate sure didn't agree with their stomachs at all. The one at the counter slowly started to back away some and at that time I felt a presence near me. I turned around and saw that large mongrel of a dog sneaking around the long counter near the front doors. That dog scared me so bad that I jumped back into the display of bags of candy shaking it a little. That made the homeless man to turn around.

"Fuck me," was all he said before the large mongrel pounced on him.

It was then I woke up from my slumber feeling a little sick to my stomach, but it soon passed. I hadn't heard anything for a few days about what happened in my dream. I was beginning to think that it was just a nightmare I had until I heard some kids stumbled upon a sight that would give them nightmares. They were playing a game of dare at that old, abandoned store when one of the boys came running out scared out of his mind. The others looked into the store after calling him a chickenshit then they too ran out. The local sheriff wasn't too pleased about what happened. What they found was a white woman laying half naked near where the cold drinks were supposed to have been and a black male laying between where that donut case used to be and the hotdog roller grill that was on that long counter. There was dried vomit where they laid and behind the woman there was a dark crusty stain on the floor and on her ass. Well, they did shit themselves in my dream. They also found body parts closer to the front as if that person was half eaten. What a dismal sight that was. From the way it looked, they been dead for a while.

7

Nothing happened for a few months as I haven't had any dreams like I had been. They were beginning to be more like nightmares to me. There were still some occasional travelers stopping by at that old store late at night and a few of them stopped here at the town to get a room for the night. A lot of the local folks in this pub get real quiet whenever some out-of-town folks talks about how nice the cashier was at that old store. What they don't know is, is that the store has been closed down and they were interacting with a ghost or spirit, if you prefer. They were decent people though otherwise they wouldn't have been here at all. A few of the folks who lives outside of town had been seeing a car go by on the roads out by that old Mercantile. Several nights the same car would go by on the back roads going by that store. Richard claimed that was the same car that parked in the lot that night when Mr. Busby was killed during that robbery. He also said that the car would drive by that old store real slow like before turning around and heading back the way it came. A few nights later I had another dream of that place.

8

No sooner I had gone to sleep I found myself just outside
next to that old green truck of Mr. Busby's. The lights within
the store were on shining through the windows out onto the
darkened parking lot. Then I heard a vehicle pulling into the
lot, parking next to the truck. The car was dark in color, I
thought it could have been a Mustang and the windows
were down, so I was able to listen to what was being said. I
knew occupants were men from the sound of their voices,
but I didn't know how many at the time.

"You're sure that's him?" asked one of the occupants.

"Yeah, I'm sure."

"Didn't you shoot him?"

"I did, I thought he was dead, bro."

"You didn't do a good job of it. It doesn't matter, he ain't
seen our faces. He doesn't know what we look like
anyways."

"You're right, are you ready to do this thing?"

"Yeah, dog."

Two individuals then stepped out of the car all clad in
black with face coverings. Before they even started toward
the front doors, I found myself inside the store standing near
the drink cooler in between the coffee bar and the hot dog
roller grill that was sitting on the long counter. At the end
of the counter by the drink cooler was a hot sandwich case
and a chili and cheese dispenser next to the hot dog roller

grill. I was standing facing the front doors to the place when I saw the two men I had seen earlier entering through the double doors and I could see that they had something in their hands, but I couldn't tell what it was until one of them pointed the object at the old man standing behind the counter next to the register.

"Don't move, old man," the guy pointing the object towards Mr. Busby yelled. It was then I knew that what they had were pistols of some kind. The other guy quickly went around the long counter passing me to Mr. Busby telling him to open the drawer of the register. The old man obliged the two and opened the drawer revealing whatever was in there. Mr. Busby was told to get back and as he did so the one at the register started grabbing what I would assume were dollar bills. The other guy looked to be a little nervous as he was looking toward the doors and back at Mr. Busby while shifting his feet. Guess he was looking out for anybody else that might happen to come in, but nobody did. What I saw next, I can't really explain too well. I will try my best to tell you what I saw. That large hairy dog materialized out of thin air as if it was coming from the floor pouncing onto the guy who was pointing his pistol at old Mr. Busby. The dog was snapping its jaws at the guy not really biting him, pushing him into the chip display stand.

The one behind the counter grabbing the cash jumped back hollering "Jesus fucking Christ! Where the fuck did that come from?"

"Shot the motherfucker!" the other yelled.

The one holding a wad of cash took his pistol and started firing it off at the mongrel. The rounds went right through the large dog and struck his partner in crime multiple times. It was a little strange as the large dog had mass to physically push the guy into the chip display stand, but the bullets just passed right through it. The one who got shot crumpled to the floor spilling the chip bags onto the ground from the display stand. I could have sworn that one of the bullets struck the guy in the head, but I'm not too sure on that.

"Fuck!" the gunman yelled. He looked over at Mr. Busby with hate in his eyes and pointed his gun towards the old man not realizing that he still had the wad of cash in his other hand. "You're dead, you fucking cracker," the gunman said to Mr. Busby. I heard a cry ring out as someone was in agonizing pain and it just so happened to be the guy holding the cash in his hand.

"Shit, shit, fuck!" was all I heard before something clattered on the floor and a loud bang rang out right after. I saw the gunman's head snap back then he fell to the ground in a heap. Shortly after, the lights within went out leaving me in darkness before I woke up from my sleep. I had heard that something had happened at that old Mercantile later that day from one of our regulars who comes in during lunchtime. The sheriff was there with his deputy for most of the day. Later that evening I heard from one of the folks who lives close to that store said that he had heard gunshots coming from that place late at night. He called the sheriff's office to get someone to check it out and one of the deputies ended up going there. During the morning hours the sheriff was there along with his deputy. Mr. Stanberg wondered over midmorning and upon seeing the sheriff, went to him.

"Shooting?" Mr. Stanberg asked.

"Yup," said the sheriff.

"Thought as much. Theirs?" Mr. Stanberg asked pointing towards a black Mustang sitting close to the store.

"Believe so."

"What are you gonna chalk it to?"

The sheriff thought it over for a moment then said, "I reckon gang related."

They were silent for a while before the sheriff spoke up saying, "What I can't figure out is how did the guy's hand got eaten with some kind of acid."

"Acid, in there?"

"Yep, fuckin' stuff ate my damn pen. Well, I'll think of somethin', I always do." Mr. Stanberg was the one who called the sheriff's office that night. He told that story when he was here at this pub later that evening about when he met the sheriff at that old Mercantile that midmorning.

9

It was a little quiet for a few days at The Mercantile. Everyone here in this town knew what was going on at that store but nobody talked about it much. Sooner or later, they knew something was gonna happen again. Even the sheriff was expecting a call which he dreaded. Those dreamless nights I had were a blessing to me. But that didn't last long at all. As you can guess, I had another one of those nightmares.

10

I had gone to bed a little earlier than normal and I wasn't asleep long before I started having those dreams. I found myself inside the store and I was alone as Mr. Busby wasn't where he usually was. I thought it strange to find him not by that register with the lights on and the shelves stocked. I was there for a few minutes before someone came in. I could tell it was a guy even though he had on a dark colored hoodie and a backpack. He walked around the store looking to see if he could see anybody while at the same time he was looking at the cigarettes behind the counter.

The guy then walked the short aisles making out like he was looking at the snacks and candy still looking for anyone else who could be in the store. Without seeing anybody else, he went across the counter and started getting quite a few packs of cigarettes putting them in the backpack. He almost got it halfway full when without warning that large dog came out of nowhere and attacked the guy. The mongrel mutt had the guy's head in its large mouth swinging him from side to side like a rag doll. Then the dog dragged the poor soul to the back of the store and was never seen again. After that the lights flickered off and I woke up.

11

It was two weeks before I had another dream and there were no mention of a missing person. I guess the guy had no one in his life who would miss him at all. He wasn't from here so that made him a lone drifter. The deputies never found out as they never went into The Mercantile. I don't believe there is a body to be found up in that store. I think the large dog took care of that. After two weeks I had another dream of that place.

12

Not long after I fell asleep, I dreamt that I was in that store. The bright florescent lights were on, and the shelves were stocked. Mr. Busby was standing where he always had been every time I had those dreams. I looked out the large bay windows expecting a car or somebody to come to the store soon. It wasn't long till I saw headlights of some vehicle pulling into the parking lot. After it had stopped, four people stumbled out of the car as if they were drunk. Two guys and two women came into the store and yep, they were drunk as they were staggering and stumbling when they entered. They were giggling about something and holding each other up trying not to fall over one another. They walked right by the old man not paying him any mind. The two women went to the hot dog roller grill while the men went straight for the alcohol. They all had to of been in their late twenties or early thirties. Not only did I see the women get some hot dogs and putting them in the buns, but they were also eating a few of them while eyeing Mr. Busby the whole time and giggling as if someone had told them a joke. The guys came around with two cases of beer and then they all went to the counter and put the stuff on there. One case of beer was Pabst Blue Ribbon, and the other was a six pack of Corona Extra. The old man looked at the stuff on the counter then at the four standing there.

"Sorry, gentlemen, I'm not able to sell you the alcohol.

It's well past midnight," Mr. Busby said.

"What? What do you mean you can't sell it?" one of the guys said. The other yelled out "That's bullshit!"

"But I want my beer," one of the girls whined. I didn't care for that whiny voice of hers. She sounded like one of those rich snobs I had dealt with before.

"You can sell it to us, we can give you cash," the first guy said.

"Sorry, I just can't sell it right now."

"You're being disrespectful, motherfucker," the second guy said then he reached for one of the bottles of Corona while knocking some items off the counter. He took the cap off then chugged the beer down.

"He threatened me. I'm going to speak to your manager, get you fired. You guys saw that didn't you," the other woman said.

"I sure did. What do you think about that, you old fuck?" the first guy said.

"My stomach hurts," the girl who had whined said while rubbing it. When I heard that, I believed that it was going to be just like what happened to the homeless people.

"What's wrong, Emily?" the other woman asked just before her stomach started bothering her too.

"Oh, fuck my stomach," she said.

The whiny woman vomited all over the floor before she could say anything. The one who downed the beer yelled, "You poisoned them, you—"

He never finished saying anything as he puked out what he drank. My guess is that he was too drunk to notice he had a problem with his gut. There was a reddish hue to the vomit and wherever that stuff landed, it started to eat what it touched as if it was acid. Both women were puking their guts out by then. One of them was holding onto the counter to keep from falling down while puking. Her legs seemed to be shaking some. The other girl was on her hands and knees up chucking all over the floor. When I looked at the guy who threw up, I saw blood with some white stuff mixed in around the guy's mouth and it looked like it was bubbling. He turned towards the other man screaming that he was hurting.

"What the fuck!" the other guy said. Then I heard what sounded like a wet fart as the women were crying and vomiting while on their hands and knees. Apparently, the woman who was trying to hold herself up went down as her legs gave up on her. Then the guy threw up again all over his buddy.

"Motherfucker!" the other guy yelled while decking his friend in the face. The other one fell on his back, and I could see bloody foam coming out of his mouth.

"It's burning me, it's burning me!" I saw the guy who got puked on trying to rub off whatever was on him, but it was no use. That stuff was burning into him and his clothes. He had gotten it on his lower jaw and down his neck and covering his shirt. He started to run while trying to rip his shirt off but tripped over the other guy's feet and went sprawling onto the floor. He withered on the ground grasping at his throat. The two women were lying on the floor and had stopped moving and I could see a lot of vomit under their heads. One of the women had a miniskirt on and I could see shit coming out as if her bowels let loose. I looked up at old Mr. Busby and he just winked at me and that was when I woke up. I was covered in sweat that morning. I heard later that day that one of the deputies rode by that Mercantile and checked out the car that was parked in the lot. The sheriff had his deputies go by there in the mornings ever since the shootings. That deputy took one look in the old store and called the sheriff. What she saw was what occurred in my dream. All four of them were on the ground dead. Both men looked like they had been eaten with some type of acid and the two women were lying in their own vomit with shit in their skirt and dress. Well, the sheriff thought of something to write in his report of what happened, but we all knew it was the spirit of Mr. Busby that caused it.

13

Two days passed before anything else happened. The sheriff was considering putting his deputies near The Mercantile to keep anyone else from going there. None of them wanted to be near that cursed place or have anything to do with it but they rode by there a few times. The local folks damn sure didn't want to have anything to do with the store, me included. They stayed away from there. Richard Bachman on the other hand did go there to visit Mr. Busby. I don't know why. A few of the folks here were saying what was happening at The Mercantile was worse than what happened to the kids who came to Playnesville in their big truck of theirs awhile back. But that's another story for another time. For those two nights only a few out of towners stopped at that old Mercantile then they were gone heading towards their destination. I don't rightly remember what it was, either some sort of event or a holiday, but there was a lot of young folks who stopped here. They were headed to some destination only they knew of. They were college kids that much I can tell you. A few of them passed by that store and got a room for the night while others went right by this town to get to where they were going, but the others stopped at that store. There were several cars in that parking lot. I started seeing some of them come into this pub before I went home. We were a little busier in this pub than usual that night because of the college students coming in here. I was sent home way before the pub closed for the night as I had to come in to get the place ready for when it opened the next day. I was dead tired that night.

14

I was asleep before my head hit the pillow and I started to dream immediately after. I found myself in that damn store next to the front entrance. The place was starting to get a little packed up in there. Most of the people were drunk from what I could tell, and they still kept coming in. I thought to myself that this was going to be worse than the previous times. I saw Mr. Busby there at the register not really doing much. It was loud and those college kids was just getting stuff they didn't really need spending money they didn't have. It seemed like they were tearing the place up getting their snacks and drinks. I glanced over at the soda fountain and saw it was a mess with cups, lids and straws on the counter by it. One thing I have never seen before was that there were totes in the aisles. There wasn't very many of them, but they looked like they had some boxes of candy and snack items. With those totes there in the aisles made it impossible for people to get around easily and it looked more packed. Those damn college kids would grab some items then decided not to get those items and just put them anywhere but where they got them from. Others were pocketing some smaller items hoping to take them without paying for them. Those college kids were like grown adult children that needed babysitting in a daycare center. That night had to be a store clerks' worst nightmare especially if they had to work it by themselves. But it didn't bother Mr.

Busby none at all, he just glanced at me and winked. I didn't understand how he was able to see me when others could not, but he was ghost after all. Not long after, Richard Bachman came in. He went to old Mr. Busby and had a little chat which I couldn't quite understand what was being said as it was a little too loud with a lot of people there. Then I saw some shady individual come into the store and started to browse the aisles looking at the items in the totes. He had a hoodie on with the hood over his head covering a ball cap and in the back pocket I saw some sort of bag protruding out. He damn sure looked like he was up to no good. Richard then left and went to the back storage room that was behind the wall where the soda fountain was set up. I didn't really notice it before but Richard left a bottle on the counter near Mr. Busby and as I looked at it, it seemed to be leaking something out of it as there was a puddle on the counter where the bottle sat. Then I saw a stream leading from the counter to where Richard went. I then glanced over and noticed that shady guy grab some boxes of candy and went the long way toward the front doors. He was having a difficult time getting there as he had to go around others and the totes. As he got there, the doors wouldn't open no matter how much he pushed or pulled which made the guy frantic. There were a few people outside trying to get in but wasn't able to get the doors open either. It was almost as if the doors were bolted shut. Then I heard a buzzing and crackling sound, then a loud pop. I looked over in the direction where Richard went and saw flames shoot out from the back storage area and licked at the substance that was on the floor running towards the counter where Mr. Busby was at. I then knew what Richard had done. He was meaning to burn the place down, but what I couldn't figure out was why now with so many people in the store. Most of the people who saw the fire yelled out and tried to get the others out of the store while trying to get to the exit themselves. Some of the others caught on fire and was trying to put out the flames. When that fire got to the counter, it went up in a blaze. At the same time the back of the store was engulfed, and the flames were spreading quickly. Those poor souls tried to break the windows but was unable to put a crack in them as those windows seemed to be bulletproof. There was a lot of screaming from those college kids, especially the ones who were caught on fire. I looked at Mr. Busby and he stood there for awhile before disappearing from sight. Before long the whole store was on fire and everyone in it was aflame. Even though the flames were all around me, I didn't feel the pain or the heat, but I did wake up jumping out of my bed looking everywhere. I realized immediately that I was in my own room and not in that Mercantile, feeling a little relief with the knowledge that maybe I won't be having any more of those dreams but a little saddened that those people had to pay a price. A part of me hoped that what I dreamt didn't really happen at all.

<h1 style="text-align: center">15</h1>

Later that morning as I got this pub ready for business, I heard that the old Mercantile burnt down. One of the women who I work with came in after I did and told me all about it. One of the deputies asked the sheriff if they should do something to save it but the sheriff's response was, "Let it burn. Let that motherfucker burn to the ground. I'm tired of the shit."

It took a while for the fire brigade to get there and by that time the store was nothing but a blazing inferno. There were plenty of people there watching it burn even some of the local folks around here. The college kids who were drunk sobered up really quick and were realizing that some of their friends were in that store burning. The place burned all night and by mornings glow the fire died down some to where the firefighters was able to put it out the rest of the way. It was an old store and the way most folks figured was that the electrical panels fried, and sparks flew onto the old wooden walls which caught fire easily. Old Richard Bachman was never seen after that day, and no one knew what became of him. Well, I know what happened to him and that store. I can tell you that I never had any of those dreams any more after that. Well, not of The Mercantile any ways. Like I said, drinks are on the house. You be careful on the road to wherever you're going. I suggest getting a room for the night as you shouldn't be driving drunk. If you're ever back by this way, I might have another story to tell you. Until then, be safe.